MAYFI...
Marie

Fred and the
Stinky Cheese

Illustrations by Bruno St-Aubin

Translated by Sarah Cummins

ormac Publishing Company Limited
Halifax, Nova Scotia 1996

Originally published as Le trésor de mon père.

Copyright © 1995 by les éditions de la courte échelle inc.

Translation copyright © 1996 by Formac Publishing Limited

Canadian Cataloguing in Publication Data

Croteau-Fleury, Marie-Danielle, 1953–

[Trésor de mon père. English]

Fred and the stinky cheese

(First novel series)

Translation of: Le trésor de mon père.

ISBN 0-88780-372-5 (pbk.) — ISBN 0-88780-373-3
(bound)

I. St-Aubin, Bruno II. Title. III. Title: Le trésor de mon
père. English. IV. Series.

PS8555.R6185T7413 1996   jC843'.54   C96-950099-8
PZ7.C76Fr 1996

Formac Publishing Limited
5502 Atlantic Street
Halifax, N.S. B3H 1G4

Printed and bound in Canada

Contents

1
One scary cheese

My father likes stinky cheese. His favourite cheese is the stinkiest of them all. It's a French cheese called *La Crotte du Diable*—the Devil's Droppings. Even the name gives away how smelly it is. But that's only half the story.

When my dad takes the cheese out of its box, strange things start to happen.

If there's a lit candle around, the flame will flicker and waver. The tablecloth wrinkles up and cutlery starts to jump around. The table legs shake.

Paintings on the wall seem to want to jump out of their frames. My goldfish swims frantically round and round in his bowl and my cat Rick starts to climb the curtains.

The cheese also has an effect on humans.

My little brother Paul, who's only one year old, turns red in the face and looks like he's choking. He lets out a loud yell and starts to cry.

My mother hurries into the kitchen to do the dishes, although usually that's my dad's job.

The Devil's Droppings sends everyone out of the room. Except my dad, of course. And me.

I love the Devil's Droppings. Not to eat—no way. This cheese is a good buddy to me.

First, it makes me laugh. Then, I get to sit alone at the dinner table with my dad. And last, this cheese once did me a big favour. Not just me, either: it helped my friend William too.

* * *

For a long while, William had been acting very strange. He'd changed. On Friday afternoon, when the final bell rang, he would get his things together and run off without even saying good-bye to me. He went back to his aunt's and I didn't hear from him until Monday morning.

I knew he spent his weekends with his dad, out on their farm. But he never called me anymore to tell me what he was doing, like he used to.

Only a few weeks earlier, we were inseparable at school. Everyone called us "the twins" or "the Siamese twins" or "the Siamese cats."

We were like brothers.

Siamese twins sometimes share an arm or a leg. Sometimes they share the whole lower part of their body.

But what William and I shared was a great, grand, extraordinary passion for animals. Especially cats.

It's partly because of William that I have a cat of my own now. Rick was born on William's farm. William took care of him and fed him until Rick came to live with me. So, in a way, William is like a father to Rick.

When your twin brother, who is also father to your beloved cat, drops you, it really hurts.

One Saturday morning I decided to tell my mom about this.

"Have you talked to William about how you feel?" she asked me.

"It's not easy! I can't even manage to get two minutes with him since Jake came to our school. It's like William is avoiding me."

"Who's Jake?"

"He's a new kid in school. Jake Doyle. He's a year older than the rest of us. His parents are making him repeat a grade because he's having trouble in English. Before they moved, he went to a French school."

"Is he nice?"

Jake Doyle was not particularly nice. Or if he was, I hadn't noticed. He didn't appeal to me and I had never tried to make friends with him, as the others had.

Everyone wanted to be his friend because he was a year older and he brought a lot of different video games to school.

In the beginning, William's reaction had been the same as mine. We thought it was stupid to spend recess pressing buttons on a little machine. We would rather play soccer or look at books about animals.

And then, I don't know what happened. William just dropped me. I was left all alone with my soccer ball, my books, and my plans of becoming a veterinarian.

"Poor Fred!" said my mom. "That must hurt."

"The worst thing is I've lost my best friend."

"But why would William not want to be your friend anymore? It doesn't make any sense. You should call him up and talk to him."

"Maybe ..."

"No maybes about it, sweetie pie. Definitely!"

"Mom! When are you going to stop calling me sweetie pie? I'm nine years old! I'm not a baby anymore."

My mom looked at me, and in her blue eyes there seemed to be a dark shadow. I must have hurt her feelings, without meaning to. I didn't even know why I had said that.

I got up and went to sit on her lap. I put my arms around her neck and hugged her tight.

She hugged me back and

stroked my hair.

"You're turning into such a big boy, Fred," she sighed.

2
Licorice whips
on the telephone

Rick and I went up to my room.

I felt a little like crying. I didn't know what was happening to me. I put Rick in his basket next to my bed and began to pet him and talk to him.

I wasn't very happy with myself. I realized that the William problem was having a big effect on me. If I didn't do something, soon even Rick wouldn't recognize me anymore. I imagined him with his claws out and his hair standing on end, treating me like a stranger.

That would be awful! I had to do something!

I went into my parents' room to call William. I closed the door and, for at least five minutes, I stared at the phone before taking the plunge. Then it took me five more minutes to raise the subject with William.

For five minutes, I twisted around like a licorice whip, chatting about this, that, and the other. I stammered out idiotic questions, winding the telephone cord around my arm.

Finally, the phone crashed to the floor. I had pulled it out of its socket.

I redialled William's number and finally asked him the question that had been gnawing at me.

"Did I do something to make you angry, William?"

There was silence. William didn't answer. Then I heard beding-bedang-clang, followed by a long paaaaaaaan. I realized that William had dropped the phone on his end, probably from twisting himself up in the cord, just like me.

What a pair of clowns! Two licorice whips tying themselves in knots. It made me giggle. When William called back, I was feeling pretty jolly. I told him the picture I had made in my mind and he laughed too.

But then he turned serious again.

"You didn't do anything to make me angry. It was Jake."

"What did he do?"

"He said that you and I are not just like twins. We're like twin sisters, always playing together like girls with their Barbie dolls. He also said that it made 'scents' that my father was a farmer. Get it?"

"You mean because you know a lot about animals?"

"Are you nuts or what? He means that I smell like a barnyard, like manure, or cow dung if you prefer."

William's voice was shaking. Jake had insulted him, but why was he taking it out on me?

"He also said that it's not normal for two boys to spend their time looking at books together."

"He did? I don't see what's wrong with it."

"Get real, Fred! All the guys in the class are making fun of us since Jake got them going. Haven't you noticed?"

I hadn't noticed anything, but I guess I hadn't been paying attention. I had been focussed on only one thing — William's attitude. Now that he pointed it out, I remembered some smirky smiles in my direction.

"We should beat Jake up for that," I said, after thinking about

it for a few seconds.

"And get expelled? My dad makes a lot of sacrifices so I can go to school in town. I had to beg him for a month before he agreed. It's hard for him. He has to spend weeks on end all alone."

William was right. He couldn't take the chance. His father had lost his wife and elder son in an accident. It was very hard for him to live apart from William. So if William were to get into trouble at school ...

"I understand, but we can't let Jake just demolish us like that, without doing anything!!"

"What do you think we should do?"

"I don't know yet. But you can be sure I'll come up with something!"

3
The cheese bell

Everything was topsy turvy. William was purring like a kitten but I felt like roaring like a lion!

I hung up and went downstairs. My mom was cooking. Paul had just stuck his hand in the butter and was getting ready to spread it all over the wall.

I caught him just in time and put him in his high chair. Then I told him what had just happened. It was easier to talk to him than to my mother. I could roar as much as I liked. It made Paul laugh and it made me feel better.

Paul was fascinated by the noises I made. He listened attentively to everything I said. That meant my mom was free to cook and listen at the same time. I thought that was pretty smart of me.

"You know, Fred, it's not easy being different."

"Who do you mean, Mom?"

"Well, William. He must be the only boy in your school who comes from the country."

After a little while, she added, "And Jake too. Put yourself in his place. Moving to a new neighbourhood, going to a new school, speaking another language. Then he has to repeat his school year and be in a class with younger kids. That's a lot! Don't you think he might need help adjusting to all that?"

"I think he needs to be taught a good lesson!"

"Don't be mean, Fred! By the way, speaking of lessons, have you done your homework? Don't forget we're having a party this evening. You'd better get your work done now, if you're planning to attend."

My parents were holding their annual cocktail party for the best customers of their fish store. My mom always prepares a feast for these occasions.

It made my mouth water just to think about it. So I went upstairs to do my homework.

When I took my notebook out of my schoolbag, a sheet of paper fell out.

Camping night at the school!

Good thing the paper fell out, otherwise I might have forgotten to get my parents to sign the permission form.

I dashed to the stairs and leaped down the first six steps before I stopped to think and—*screeech*—put on the brakes.

Did I still want to go to this camping party, given everything that was going on in school lately?

I went back upstairs. I wasn't at all sure I did want to.

I opened my math book and got to work. Talk about problems!

One: I go, and maybe I'll be teased. Two: I don't go and everyone picks on me the next morning. Three: I go, but maybe William doesn't go, and I'm bored all by myself.

I closed the book and stretched out on the bed.

Four: I don't go, William goes, and he's the one left all alone. Five: both William and I go. Either he won't want to hang around with me, or else we'll stick together and then—

"Fred? Fred, are you asleep? My goodness! Our guests are already here! Get a move on!"

"Huh? What? What guests?"

I opened one eye, then the other, and I saw my father. He was shaking me like a plum tree. I got up and followed him downstairs. But I didn't really wake up until I got to the table.

Wow! Paté, all kinds of bread and rolls, pink, yellow, and green mousse, mountains of shrimp, and tons of crab legs.

And right in the middle of the cheese tray, a little glass dome. And underneath the glass was my father's treasure, his little trick for bringing the party to a close: the Devil's Droppings.

When my dad lifted up the glass, it would be like a bell signalling the end. The guests would make their excuses and sidle towards the door. *Thank you. Thank you so much. It was*

lovely, but it's late now and we must leave.

My dad winked at me. He, my mom, and I were the only ones who knew about this secret plan.

4
My secret weapon

It was settled: I would go camping with my class, and William was going to come too. On Sunday I called him and told him that I had come up with a brilliant idea. We would use the camping night in the gym to teach Jake a good lesson. A lesson that wouldn't hurt him in any way, but one he would remember for a long, long time.

Of course, William was dying to know what I was planning to do.

"You promise not to laugh?"

"Cross my heart and hope to die. I spit on it."

The poor telephone!

When I explained my idea, William burst out laughing. He laughed!

Finally, he said, "That's a great idea, Fred! I'll go along with it, on one condition. From now until camping night, forget you even know me."

William didn't want things to get any worse over the next week. If Jake thought we were plotting against him, he might turn nasty.

"You never can tell. After all, we don't know him very well."

William was right to be careful. And he was definitely right to say we didn't know Jake very well.

But we would get to know him better over the next weekend ...

On Friday morning I got up early to pack my bags. Then I went down to breakfast. A bowl of cereal was waiting for me on the table, next to my lunchbag. My mom was busy with Paul and my dad was taking a shower.

I seized the opportunity to prepare the ammunition for my secret weapon.

I opened the fridge and took out a piece of the Devil's Droppings. Perfect! The cheese was very ripe. It would really stink when it reached room temperature.

For the time being, it wasn't too bad because it was cold. I quickly put it in a little jar, and put the jar next to the cooler in my lunch box.

Then I kissed everyone good-bye. That is, everyone but Rick. When I reached out to pet him, he hissed. His fur stood on end and he ran away.

"What's the matter with him?" my mother worried.

"He's sad that I'm leaving ..."

I was certainly not going to say it was because my hands smelled. But Rick's behaviour made me realize that I had better wash my hands before I left.

I wanted everyone to say that Jake Doyle smelled like a barn-yard, not me!

5
Camping night

At noon, I didn't dare open my lunch box. Fortunately I had stuffed an apple in my coat pocket just before leaving home.

In any case, I wasn't hungry. Like all the other kids, I was excited. It was carnival day and there were special activities in all the classes.

Finally the bell rang. We picked up our stuff and went down to the gym to watch a play. What a surprise to see Jake Doyle stop at his locker, take out his coat, and leave!

"Darn!" I whispered in William's ear. "I didn't think of that!"

Jake wasn't going to camp with us!

"It's perfect," William answered.

I didn't agree, I wanted to settle the problem with Jake once and for all.

I watched the play without really paying attention. Even the three-horned devil on stage didn't make me laugh.

Everyone else, though, was splitting their sides every time the devil opened his mouth. He breathed smoke and his voice was totally inhuman. It was as if he was speaking from inside a metal box.

It didn't make me laugh, but I

did wonder who was playing the devil and how he did his tricks.

Jake Doyle! The devil was Jake Doyle! When he took off his mask at the end, all the kids in my class gave him a standing ovation.

Jake had kept his secret well. No one knew that he was an actor. You can imagine how popular he was when he joined the rest of the class for dinner. Everyone was at his beck and call.

"Milk, please."

Seven cartons of milk landed in front of him.

Only William and I, one at each end of the table, ignored him while we ate our meal.

This seemed to bother Jake. He kept on making jokes and looking at us to see our reaction.

It was as if he was putting on a show just for the two of us.

But William and I paid no attention. William read a comic book and I just ate my spaghetti. I felt nervous and distracted. I hoped I wouldn't fall asleep before I could put my plan into action.

After dinner, there was a fun fair. Then we watched a movie, and finally we got ready for bed.

I thought the hardest part of my plan would be to get my sleeping bag next to Jake's, because everyone wanted to be next to him. But I managed! While the others were arguing about it, I quickly slipped in and unrolled my sleeping bag.

When they turned around, my head was already on the pillow.

Jake seemed to think it was a pretty clever move. He gave me a look as if to say, "What a

bunch of babies!"

I almost began to think he was nice. I was nearly ready to give up my plan.

But unfortunately for him, Jake couldn't help adding his own two cents' worth when Nate said, "Too late, guys. The Siamese has taken the spot."

"The Siamese kitty cat!" said Jake.

They all began to meow like a bunch of fools. They made so much noise the teacher got mad. But nobody paid any attention to her, so she turned out the lights. I took advantage of the resulting confusion to put my plan into effect.

6
A keen-nosed teacher

I had hidden my lunch box in my backpack. I quickly took out the cheese, which was still cold. With a knife I gently set the piece of the Devil's Droppings in one of Jake's shoes.

It wasn't long before the stink hit the fan.

By the time the teacher had quieted everyone down, the cheese had warmed up. The smell began to waft through the gymnasium.

"Yikes! Put your socks back on, Nate!"

"It's not me! It's coming from

the other side of the room!"

"Quiet, children!"

"But Mrs. Mantell, someone's done it in his pants!"

"Yuck!"

"That's enough, I said! It's time to go to sleep now."

Mrs. Mantell had lost control of the situation. She turned the lights back on, and at that second, the smell hit her.

"Heavens! What is that? Come on, children, everyone get over here."

The kids all huddled in one corner of the gym and Mrs. Mantell tried to figure out where the smell was coming from. It was so funny to watch her! She tiptoed here and there, raising her nose and sniffing like a police dog.

We were all killing ourselves laughing. Especially William. He laughed so hard he cried. And he came over to stand next

to me. He didn't care what the others said. I had won!

That is, I thought I had won ...

Mrs. Mantell was getting closer and closer to the cheese. Next to Jake's sleeping bag she picked up his shoe and dangled it by the lace, holding her nose.

"Whose shoe is this?"

After a long silence, Jake answered, "Mine!"

He had turned as red as his devil costume.

"That's why it smells like the devil!" cracked Nate.

All of the kids edged away from Jake as if they were afraid of catching some disease.

Once they had moved away, they started to make jokes. The same jokes that Jake had made about William, concerning barnyard smells and farmers.

I felt uneasy, but Jake had asked for it. His jokes were coming back to haunt him. Served him right!

"Quiet, children!" cried Mrs. Mantell. "I have another question."

She bent down and put the shoe on the floor. When she straightened up again, she was holding something else high in the air.

"Jake," she asked, "does this belong to you, too?"

7
A present from the devil

If Jake had turned red, then I must have turned purple.

Mrs. Mantell was something else. It hadn't taken her two minutes to sniff out my lunch box and the jar.

"Well, Fred, I see you're quite the gourmet."

"What is it, Mrs. Mantell?" asked Jake, looking at me.

"Ask Fred. It's a present from him."

I was so embarrassed! I didn't know what to do with myself.

"Well, I'll tell you what it is," said Mrs. Mantell. "It's the

Devil's Droppings. An excellent imported cheese. Its only drawback is that it doesn't smell very good. As you can tell."

I could tell that Mrs. Mantell was trying hard not to laugh out loud. But Jake didn't hold back.

"The Devil's Droppings! That's a good one! The devil did a dump in his shoe!"

Jake couldn't stop laughing. Mrs. Mantell had to raise her voice and send us all back to bed before he calmed down.

"I want you to come see me after camping night, Fred. We'll talk about this matter then. You too, Jake. I have something I want to tell you."

I didn't sleep very well. I wasn't worried about Mrs. Mantell. Usually she is very nice and even funny. But I was afraid of Jake's reaction. I had made a fool of myself in front of the whole class. I would be an easy target for him now.

On the way to Mrs. Mantell's office the next day, I ran into Jake. He looked pitiful. When he saw me, he lowered his head and kept on walking, staring at his shoes.

"Come in and sit down," said Mrs. Mantell. "As you can see, the seat is still warm. Your friend Jake warmed it for you."

She had a strange little smile on her face. I really didn't know what to expect.

"Jake's not my friend. He insulted William."

"And you wanted to get even ... I know all that."

"How do you know?"

"I'm not blind. I could tell what Jake was up to at recess. And there was a reason I asked him to come see me before you. I had my own idea about his behaviour and I wanted to see if I was right."

"What was your idea?"

Mrs. Mantell explained that, although Jake didn't even realize it, deep down he was jealous of William and me. He envied us, our friendship, and our passion for cats.

"He would love to have a cat himself. But his parents are dead set against it."

"How come?"

"Oh, you know, cat hairs, claw marks, cat diseases ... And his parents own a bakery and the shop is right next to their kitchen. They're afraid the cat will make a mess in the bakery, you understand?"

Did I understand! This was exactly what I went through at home, with our fish store! I told this to Mrs. Mantell.

"Oh really? And you managed to change your parents' minds?"

"It took a long time, but they finally agreed."

"That's great, Fred. For your punishment, you will go see Jake on Monday at recess and you will tell him what you did to change their minds."

"But, Mrs. Mantell, how can I go talk to him? I just saw him and he wouldn't even look at me."

"Well, I was pretty hard on him. But don't worry. He's going to think it over. He is a very intelligent boy. I think we can count on him. In fact, you may be hearing from him before Monday."

"What makes you say that?"

Mrs. Mantell raised her nose in the air, and said, "Let's just say I have a good nose, Fred."

Well, from what I had seen the previous evening, I didn't doubt her. But I could not have imagined what would happen next.

I went back to the gym. Jake had left, so I decided to stay and play a little basketball.

Around four o'clock, I picked up my sleeping bag and my backpack and headed home.

When I got there, my mom said that someone had just left something for me in the fish store.

"What is it?"

"I don't know. Go see!"

My father had stowed the package on the floor underneath the cash register.

"I hope it's not a bomb!" I joked.

Well, it was a bomb. A stink bomb. A whole wheel of Devil's Droppings cheese, very ripe.

"That's strange," said my dad, when he saw the cheese. "There must be some mistake. This can't be for you. I wonder who ... Oh, look! There's an envelope."

He picked up the envelope from where it had fallen on the floor, and opened it.

"This gets stranger and stranger."

"What does it say, Dad?"

"It just says, 'From Beelzebub.' "

"Who's Beelzebub?"

"The devil ..."

I put on my most innocent look and told my dad, "You're

probably right. It must be for you."

So my dad had a devil of a mystery to solve. I went up to my room, thinking that Mrs. Mantell was a real treasure. Funny, understanding, with a terrifyingly sharp nose!

Not only had I heard from Jake, but in record time too.

Suddenly a lightbulb went on in my head. This was surely Mrs. Mantell's idea! A punishment for Jake, it was also a way to bring us together.

Well, it had worked! I couldn't wait for Monday to come. I was looking forward to meeting the devil again and finding out that he was not ... The Kid from Hell.